THREE CLASSIC CHILDREN'S STORIES

DRAWINGS BY Edward Gorey
TEXT BY James Donnelly

THREE CLASSIC CHILDREN'S STORIES

DRAWINGS BY **Edward Gorey**
TEXT BY **James Donnelly**

LITTLE RED RIDING HOOD

JACK the GIANT-KILLER

RUMPELSTILTSKIN

Pomegranate **Kids**®
SAN FRANCISCO

Published by Pomegranate Communications, Inc.
Box 808022, Petaluma, CA 94975
800.227.1428 | www.pomegranate.com

Pomegranate Europe Ltd.
Unit 1, Heathcote Business Centre, Hurlbutt Road
Warwick, Warwickshire CV34 6TD, UK
[+44] 0 1926 430111 | sales@pomeurope.co.uk

This edition first published by Pomegranate Communications, Inc., 2010.

Library of Congress Cataloging-in-Publication Data
Donnelly, James (James Kevin), 1952–
   Three classic children's stories : Little Red Riding Hood, Jack the
giant killer, Rumpelstiltskin / drawings by Edward Gorey ; text by
James Donnelly.
      p. cm.
   Summary: Puts a new twist on three classic fairy tales, as Little Red,
her grandmother, and the woodcutter are rewarded, Jack taunts the
last remaining giant in Cornwall, and Omoline, the miller's daughter,
toys with the ugly little man who wants to take her child.
   ISBN 978-0-7649-5546-4 (hardcover)
1. Fairy tales. 2. Children's stories, American. [1. Fairy tales. 2.
Short stories.] I. Gorey, Edward, 1925–2000, ill. II. Title.
PZ8.D7318Thr 2010
[E]—dc22

2010011197

Pomegranate Catalog No. A188
Designed by Harrah Lord, Rockport, Maine

Printed in China

19 18 17 16 15 14 13 12 11 10   10 9 8 7 6 5 4 3 2 1

CONTENTS

LITTLE RED RIDING HOOD

DRAWINGS BY **Edward Gorey**

TEXT BY **James** Donnelly &
Cecily Donnelly

There once was a girl who lived with her mother in a cottage at the edge of a great dark forest. She went about in a bright red cloak, with a useful hood to keep the rain off her head. For this reason, nearly everyone called her Little Red Riding Hood.

One day Little Red Riding Hood's mother said,

"Dearie, your old granny is feeling unwell, and she has been having trouble sleeping. Come, put on your hood, and take this poppy cake to her, and this little pot of valerian jam." Little Red Riding Hood's mother knew poppy cake and valerian jam to be excellent remedies for sleeplessness.

She continued, "You know the way to her house in the forest; but see that you keep to the path. Don't wander. Don't dally and don't dream. Don't take shortcuts. And keep yourself to yourself."

Little Red Riding Hood was of an age to be slightly impatient with instructions. "For babies," she thought. "Mother! I've been to Granny's before," she thought. But she was not yet of an age to say these things aloud.

It is true that Little Red Riding Hood had gone often to Granny's, but always with her mother. Granny's cottage was not very far away, but the path took many twists and turns; it could be hard to follow in the deep, dark shadow of the forest. The journey could seem unduly long to a small (though stalwart) girl.

A good way into the woods, Little Red Riding Hood paused to rest and to enjoy the local sounds—birds boldly cheeping, squirrels busily scrabbling—and the cool perfume of pine duff, leaf mold, and the shy forest flowers: woodbine, may apple, wild turnip.

There came a new sound: a padding footstep, soft but heavy, careful yet clumsy. The sound drew near.

WHUMP and a minor cloud of dust! Something leapt into the path. Little Red Riding Hood hastily arose, and her eyes met the curious gaze of a great gray wolf.

Little Red Riding Hood had heard her share of wolf stories—how the sleigh carrying Count Mazurka and all his gold had been found, horseless and Countless, overturned in the snow among a welter of sharp-clawed pawprints; how Lame Edgar's beard turned white overnight while he clung terrified to a high branch, the Black Mountain pack gazing hungrily up at him till dawn. But here and now, above the forest's perpetual twilight, the noonday sun was blazing; she was heartened by its comforting presence.

Furthermore, Little Red Riding Hood had never heard of a wolf that went marauding on two legs, upright as herself; or one that smiled such a friendly smile. Or spoke:

"Good day to you, little dear. (Would you say you were meaty, or scant?) What fortune to find ourselves on this fine broad well-lit well-traveled path! (About forty, fifty pounds, are you?) Shall we walk along together for a bit of company? I'm only going as far as—" (Here the wolf muttered inaudibly.)

"And I am taking poppy cake and jam to my granny's. The little yellow house in a clearing, do you know it? About a mile—or a half-mile, or a mile and a half—down this path." Little Red Riding Hood recalled her mother's instructions. "But I am to keep myself to myself. Lovely to meet you, though, I'm sure. Goodbye now!"

"In truth," replied the wolf, "I, too, enjoy a solitary stroll. The better to appreciate this excellent forest: so deep and dark, so vast, so lonely! But here's a word to the wise (I see you *are* a wise, and also perhaps a sturdy, even a plump, little girl).

"Not a quarter-mile from here," the wolf continued, "is a sunny clearing; and there grow flowers of a crimson to rival your own red cloak. And from there you can walk but a little way to the west and find the path again. It's as good as short ribs—I mean, as a shortcut! I suggest you pick some pretty bonny flowers for your grandma."

Little Red Riding Hood gave this idea some thought.

She was not a timid girl—far from it—but her life so far had scarcely tested her bravery.

Also, she was a proud girl.

"Granny will be so pleased," she thought, "and Mama so impressed. This shows real maturity!"

She thought she needn't mention that the flowers were the wolf's idea. Nor, indeed, that she had met a wolf and spoken with him. Why give Mama and Granny cause to worry?

Finding the flowery clearing just where the wolf said it would be, Little Red Riding Hood set about picking a fine bouquet. She did not see the wolf as he hastened down the path to Granny's cottage.

While Little Red Riding Hood picked flowers, the great gray wolf—no true friend to man or girl—made his way to Granny's. He went awkwardly on his hind legs, but no one could convince him that his upright posture lacked elegance.

He knocked gently at the cottage door.

"Who's there?" came Grandmother's voice, age-worn but sweet.

The wolf chafed his forepaws one against the other. He swallowed several times. This would be the worst—or, in wolf terms, the best—wickedness of his long and hideous career; for what he had in mind was a two-course meal followed by a poppy-cake dessert. Too bad, he thought, that he would have to have the main course first and the appetizer second!

Coaxing his voice into a horrid falsetto, he squeaked like a balloon:

"'Tis I, poor dear ailing helpless old Grandmama: Little Red Riding Hood, with a basket of treats. Open up!"

Granny was a little nettled by this brash greeting. She was also mildly alarmed by Little Red Riding Hood's new harsh voice. But of course she loved her granddaughter, brash or not; and she really was ill, and didn't much want to clamber out of bed and peek discreetly at her visitor through a door-crack; and so she replied,

"Come in, come in, my dear; do come in."

The wolf required no further invitation.

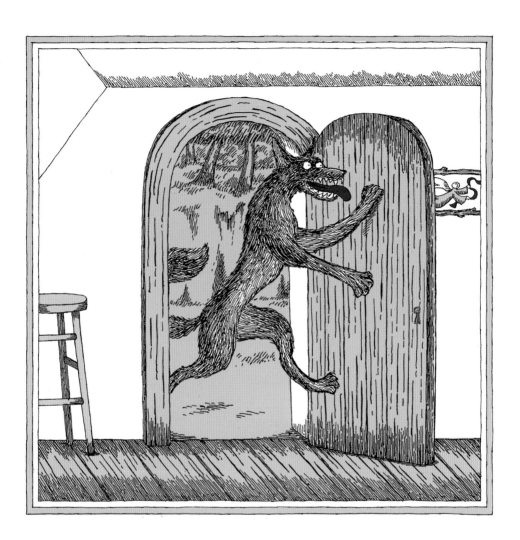

In a flurry of unspeakable glee and gluttony,
the wicked beast swallowed Granny whole with a
great gargling gulp whose echoes set the crockery
wobbling on its shelves. Thinking regretfully "I
must try to remember to chew my victims," he
spat out her linen bedcap, her spectacles, and
the novel she had been reading. He put on the
cap and the eyeglasses. He glanced at the book—a
potboiler called *The Teacosy Crime*, by D. Awdrey-
Gore—and tossed it aside. And then he leapt into
Granny's bed and pulled the coverlet up to his
bristly snout.

"Perhaps *I* should write a book," he thought,
contented. "My memoirs. So that less
accomplished fiends might learn from my
glorious, my exemplary deeds of mayhem."
The wolf yawned hugely. "Must stay alert.
No time for a nap."

All was now ready for the second course.

Little Red Riding Hood found the door open.

Grandmother *did* look ill.

"Hello, Granny! I've brought you a poppy cake to help you sleep, and a pot of valerian jam, also to help you sleep. And a big red bouquet picked by myself."

"Come here, dear child," rasped the wolf, "and let me look at you. Closer, closer—confound these old spectacles!"

The wolf squinted at Little Red Riding Hood through spit-smeared eyeglasses, and Little Red Riding Hood squinted back.

"Why, Grandmother," she said. "What big, smeary eyes you have!"

"The better to see you with, except for these—oof!—these spectacles. Oof! Ow!" Deep in the wolf's red stomach, eaten but unbeaten, Granny was kicking and elbowing. "Urp! Agh!" Granny stepped on the wolf's kidneys.

Little Red Riding Hood looked sidelong at the gnarled, callused feet that protruded from beneath the coverlet. "What ugly slippers!" she thought, but politely did not say.

"What big strong hairy hands you have, Grandmother!" An icy trickle of doubt and dread began its slow journey down Little Red Riding Hood's spine.

"The better, ugh!, to hug you with, *ow*, OUCH, dearie," the gray wolf replied. A little glowing ball of outrage formed in the girl, overcoming her fear.

"And, Grandmother, what great long yellow teeth you have!"

"The better—OUCH! Dang!—to eat yOOF!—to eaUGH! *Ow!* To, to eat you up!"

And the wolf sprang from the bed, his jaws snapping like castanets.

But Little Red Riding Hood did not hold still to be gobbled. She jinked to the left and she juked to the right, and from her basket she withdrew the valerian jam in its little stone pot; and this she threw, arrow-straight, into the wolf's greedy maw.

He crunched it up.

Little Red Riding Hood then hurled the poppy cake. This missile, too, caught the wolf square in the mush. "Delicious!" he cried.

And paused in his pursuit.

As Little Red Riding Hood scrambled under the bed, she heard the wolf yawn. "Such a fine cake . . . and the jam, with the crunchy bits in it . . . excellent, excellent . . . Feeling a trifle sleepy, I am." Little Red Riding Hood crawled to the corner farthest from the wolf. "Perhaps a little rest . . . Job well done, the second course can wait . . . And this time I'll remember to chew . . . "

Asleep on his feet, the wolf toppled backward upon the bed.

Within the cottage, the sleeping wolf drooled on Grandmother's pillow. Within the wolf, Granny sensed a change of circumstances and ceased to pinch his vitals. Little Red Riding Hood crawled with great care from under the bed.

Outside, the wildwood rang to the wolf's guttural, golloping snores. A woodcutter, ambling the forest in search of deadfallen trees, heard and approached. Little Red Riding Hood scurried out to meet him.

"... And so, and so, he ate my grandma, the great pig—at least I think he did—and furthermore he tried to *fool me!* And for that I *will not stand!*" Little Red Riding Hood scarcely had time to finish explaining the situation before the woodcutter took action. He had been longing all day to cut something.

"Careful, oh, careful!" whispered Little Red Riding Hood. The woodcutter wielded his dagger with a surgeon's delicacy. In a moment he had opened the slumbering wolf like a cheap, hairy suitcase. Granny stuck her head out and looked about her; then, embarrassed, she fled to the pantry for a quick sponge-bath and a change of nightgown. Little Red Riding Hood regathered her bouquet, aware that she might have some explaining to do.

"Oh, my dear, my dearest dear," said Granny, stroking the fierce little head beneath the hood. "The woodcutter got you out," muttered Little Red Riding Hood, "but he was acting at my direction." Behind them, the woodcutter, still rummaging in the wolf, gave a whistle of astonishment.

"Come here to me, ladies," he called, "and help me look at this!"

To spare them another, and even less appealing, view of the wolf, he brought forth the two great sacks he had extracted from the creature's innards. Each sack bore the Mazurka crest—the ancient crest of a family long vanished and gone—and each clinked promisingly when the woodcutter jostled it.

And indeed, the sacks contained the gold that had disappeared when the luckless Count Mazurka was devoured, many years before. "What a careless wanton wolf!" said Granny. "*Lupus gluttonus,* for a fact," said the woodcutter. "Are we rich?" asked Little Red Riding Hood.

The grown-ups looked at one another with dawning joy. "Yes," said Grandmother. "Yes, we're rich: you and me and this good man, and your mother, and her neighbors, and the whole village if you like."

Granny hated disorder and mess. She took a few quick stitches in the wolf "to tidy him up."

The woodcutter said, "My first purchase will be a medal for this dauntless girl."

Grandmother said, "Mine will be a new coverlet, I think. A new pillow, too."

"And I," said Little Red Riding Hood, "shall have this wicked wolf stuffed, in an attitude so frightening as to freeze the blood in one's veins, and he can be in my room, and I'll hang my medal on him when I take it off at night."

But, being grown-ups, they talked her out of that idea. And she conceded that it was perhaps a little childish, which certainly didn't reflect her true self.

The woodcutter used that wolfskin for many years, to carry bundles of wood from the forest; and people who saw it were reminded of just who he was.

Granny said, "I think we'll walk back to your mother's now, and in the morning we can tell the village that everyone is rich." They returned to the house at the forest's edge where Little Red Riding Hood lived with her mother, and Mama said, "Brave girl! O great heart!" and wept. And Granny fell fast asleep and awoke the next morning looking healthy and pink.

And Little Red Riding Hood got her medal, and wore it for a few days before she lost it in the creek. And she grew up to do important things, things that required both great bravery and excellent judgment.

JACK THE GIANT-KILLER

DRAWINGS BY
Edward Gorey

TEXT BY
James Donnelly

The boy Jack.

The giant Gawr.

L ong ago—before King Arthur, and even before the Romans ruled—Britain was home to a race of giants. Over hundreds of years, men battled these giants, driving them ever northward: into the Borders, into Scotland, finally into the North Sea, where they drowned.

All but one: A wily giant named Gawr hid himself on a lonely island near the Cornish coast and let the battles go on without him.

Centuries passed. Gawr became intolerably
hungry. Finally, lured by the smoke of cookstoves
and the sight of distant sheep nibbling the
mainland turf, he waded across the shallow
channel to Cornwall.

Now, life was not easy for the people who lived
along the coast. Summer was short, winter long,
and the west wind blew all year. Those who
stayed were hardy and capable and tough. But
no one had bargained for a starving giant.

Once ashore, Gawr snatched up sheep and ate them by the fistful, pushing their scratchy wool down his throat with an acre or two of green hay. Passing an abbey, he plucked up and devoured a monk distracted by prayer; then he ate the abbot's milch cow, and then he ate the abbot. He ran his cracked yellow fingernails the length of a turnip field, harvesting the crop in one swipe. He pulled the thatch off a cottage and gobbled two little girls he found inside it. At nightfall he waded home to his soft bed of shredded trees.

This became a regular amusement for the giant. Every few days he filled his belly with Cornish men, women, children, and livestock; between raids he slept sweetly on his island.

Of the many tough residents of that windblown
coast, the toughest was a lad named Jack. No
one, not even he himself, knew this fact until
the giant came along; people took Jack for just
another stubborn, half-wild Cornwall boy.

Chaos ruled Jack's village. The wisest heads had
been swallowed; the fields were despoiled; no
moo, no baa, no birdsong could be heard. From
their hiding places, the townsfolk kept watch on
the giant's island and listened fearfully for his
approach. Jack resolved to end Gawr's reign
of gluttony.

In a shattered cottage, Jack found a shovel and
a long tin trumpet. (He had hoped for a sword.)
As night fell, his tools tied over his shoulder, he
walked down to the water, where the outgoing
tide bore him to the giant's island.

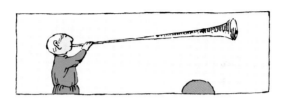

Half-frozen, Jack warmed himself by digging
a great pit: a giant-size pit that took him all night.
A monstrously deep pit, which he covered with
brush. At dawn he took the horn in his blistered
hands and blew a loud, rude, taunting blast.

The last time Gawr had heard such a note, it had come with an army of tiny but ferocious men who slew his comrades. Wild-eyed, he leaped up. He was clumsy and smelly and oafish; his breath was awful and his beard was full of skulls and worse; but he was no coward, and he had a grievance. Gawr slapped his pockets to be sure he had his salt and his pepper; then, plucking a tall fir tree for a club, he galloped toward the sneering bleat of Jack's tin horn.

Where he had expected to find a hundred
armed men he found but one small boy who
capered mockingly on the shore. "Come, giant!"
cried Jack. "Here, Lumpy!" *Blaart! Bwceent!*—Jack
blew his horn. "I shall have him in two steps,"
thought Gawr. "And then we'll see about this
Lumpy business."

But he took *one* step, and the ground fell away
beneath him, and he tumbled, OOF, into Jack's
giant-trap. Jack stepped up smartly and swung
his shovel: WHANG.

Every giant had a soft spot at the top of his otherwise rocklike head. Jack happened to hit Gawr right on the soft spot, and with that one lucky blow he killed the last of the giants. He then filled in the trap with a few shovelfuls of sand; and, climbing to the top of the very large hill of leftover dirt and rocks, he planted the horn there as a marker. Jack knew his tides; he let the ocean carry his tired body inshore, arriving by breakfast time.

Up and down the Cornwall coast, people had been startled from their hiding places by the rude dawn song of Jack's tin trumpet. Looking to the distant island, they saw Gawr raging and brandishing a tree; then, suddenly, they saw him no more. Hope arose among them as the sun rose behind them.

Now they cheered as the boy emerged from
the waves.

And didn't they make much of him when Jack
told his story! Flags flew over the trampled cliffs.
Towns were rebuilt and people got on with
their lives.

Young Jack grew to be as wise as he was brave,
and he was respected and listened to all over
Cornwall. Wherever they traveled, his neighbors
(truthfully or not) claimed kinship with the
fearless lad.

Which is why, if
you're ever looking
for a Cornishman,
you have but to
mention Cousin
Jack.

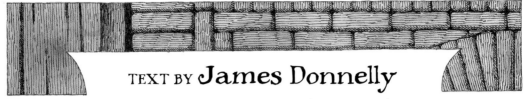

TEXT BY **James** Donnelly

RUMPELSTILTSKIN

DRAWINGS BY **Edward Gorey**

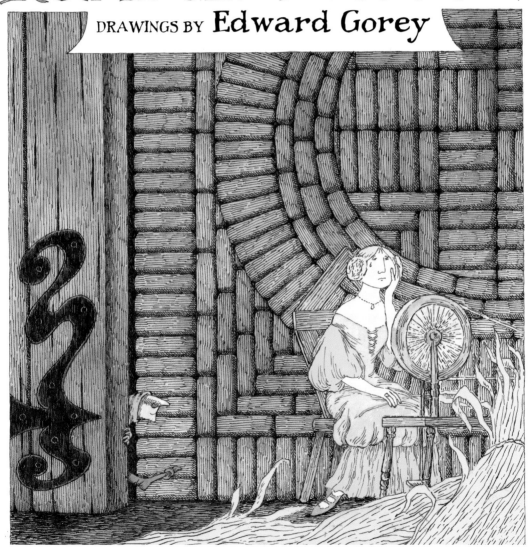

Down by the river lived a miller. He had little money and less respect for the truth, but he did have a beautiful daughter. Her name was Omoline.

One day the king came riding along. He was young and had only recently become the king, and he, too, had little money (for a king). In fact, his purpose that morning was to collect taxes from his subjects.

"Ho, miller!" cried the king. "Do you prosper?"

The miller knew where this question would lead. "No, Sire, I am completely impoverished—" The king scowled. "But, but," the miller stammered, "my daughter here can spin gold from ordinary straw!" Omoline looked around to see if her father was talking about some other, more talented daughter.

"Huh!" The king tugged his moustache. "Straw into gold?" The miller wished he had kept his mouth shut. "Well, send her along to my castle. I have quite a lot of straw." And he spurred his big bay horse and cantered away.

The words that then passed between Omoline
and her father may as well not be repeated. It is
enough to say that she presented herself before
the king that evening.

The king (whose name was Leonino) was smitten
by her beauty. He gulped and swallowed hard,
feeling his heart swell like a comic valentine. But
a king cannot rule without a treasury, and
Leonino's treasury was the subject of unpleasant
jokes among his creditors; and so he took
Omoline to a little windowless candlelit room.

In the room were a stool and a spinning-wheel
and a heap of straw. "Now," said the king, "spin.
Make me some gold before the morning comes.
And if you don't—" Trying to make light of his
threat, he crossed his eyes as he drew a finger
across his throat. But Omoline took the gesture
very seriously, as well she might.

The king locked her in. Bewildered and afraid,
she began to cry.

As if summoned by her unhappiness, a little misshapen manikin appeared. "A gnome, perhaps," thought Omoline, "or an unsightly class of elf."

"Evening, Miss Miller," he rasped. "Why the tears?"

"O little man! I must spin straw into gold or die!"

"Hm! Spinning happens to be a particular talent of mine. But why should I do it for you?"

Omoline offered him her necklace of amber. The little man gave it a brief, appraising look and put it in his pocket; then he sat down at the wheel and turned it gently. At his direction, the

miller's daughter twisted up hanks of straw and
gave them, just so, to the little man. Humming a
strange, disjointed tune, he fed the straw onto the
wheel with his left hand while spinning it with his
right. A strand of something like yarn—like yarn,
but with a bright metallic luster—began to wind
itself around the spindle.

Well before dawn, the room was empty of straw.
A great skein of twisted gold filled one corner.
The little man receded into another, darker
corner, and when Omoline turned to thank him
she found him altogether gone.

Leonino had spent a bad night. Being king brought duties for which he lacked enthusiasm. Could he really be expected to kill a young woman for failing at an impossible task? Imagine, then, his delight to find the straw converted to gold!

He was shaking Omoline's hand, and wondering if he dared give her a little kiss—a strictly official kiss of royal gratitude—when his accountant came up and whispered in his ear. The king frowned.

"It appears I must have more treasure than this," he told the girl ruefully. "We'll have a good breakfast, and you'll have a day's rest, and then I'm afraid you'll have to spin gold again."

Evening came. Preparing to lock Omoline in with her wheel and straw, Leonino found he couldn't bear to threaten her with death. So instead he commanded, "Spin, or I'll take away your father's mill"—not that he wanted a mill, or, really, much of anything except to see the miller's daughter smile. But he dutifully locked her in.

If her father lost his mill, the old liar would probably expect her to support him for the rest of his life. Omoline found this prospect so dismal that she began to weep.

"What cheer, milady! Why the waterworks?"
The ugly little man was back, and in good humor.
"Straw into gold for you again, I expect. And what
for me?" This time Omoline offered him her ring.
"Only garnet, and chipped," he sniffed. "But
it'll do."

The night passed as before. By daybreak a coil of pure spun gold half-filled the room, and the little man had disappeared.

King Leonino was pleased beyond measure.
This time he seized Omoline's hand and kissed
it. They both blushed. But the king's counselors
came bustling down the corridor; weighing the
gold with their eyes, they looked at one another
unhappily. One took Leonino's sleeve and
murmured to him. "Oh, surely not," said the king.

He sorrowfully informed Omoline that her work
must resume when darkness fell.

By now the king was well and truly in love with his lovely subject, and he had resolved to rule with a gentler hand than tradition demanded. And so, at the door to the room with the stool and wheel and, tonight, an enormous pile of straw, he said:

"Spin, my dear, and fill my treasury! And if you do, I'll make you my bride, my Queen Omoline!" He paused, looking a little foolish. "If, I mean, I, if you want me to . . ." Leonino really hadn't gotten the hang of being king yet.

Omoline thought it prudent to look happy and keep silent. But when she was locked in the mean, comfortless room, doubt and dread overtook her. Reluctant tears stood, scalding, in her eyes.

Cheerier than ever, the small twisted man came capering out of the shadows. He danced a music-hall shuffle and sang:

> "I can spin gold like a chicken lays an egg,
> But my mother told me never work for free.
> I can make a queen of my little Omoline
> If she'll only do a little thing for me.
>
> "Ev'ry favor has its price,
> O wouldn't you agree?
> I can put a throne under little Ee-molone
> If she'll give a little thing to me."

He kicked and twirled and sank with an odd grace onto the stool. "What'll it be tonight, girl?" Omoline gave no sign that she disliked overfamiliar talk from gnomes. "Do a deal, shall we? What have you to trade for my services?"

Now, Omoline had no more jewelry, not even a pretty shell; her shoes were cracked and broken, her dress a much-patched hand-me-down.

"O good Sir Gnome, I've nothing left to interest you!" Her tears overflowing, she put her head in her hands and sobbed.

"'Sir Gnome'—I like that, I do. But here, stop blubbering. I'll help you, for I've a big heart: ask anyone. Just promise me now and pay me later!" The little man proffered a dubious handkerchief. "Here, blow!"

"Pay you—sniff!—pay you *what* later, exactly?" Omoline hastily blotted her tears on her own sleeve.

"A little thing. So to speak. A trifle only." And
he sang,

> "Pretty girl from down the mill,
> I'll take your baby Under the Hill.
> When you are Queen I'll call one day,
> And fetch your firstborn far away."

It was getting late. And the straw was still straw.
And Omoline was only a girl, and she could
scarcely imagine that she might ever become a
queen—let alone that she might bear the king's
child—in fact she found babies a little boring, and
had no plans to have one herself. And so she
agreed: "Spin, then, Sir Gnome!"

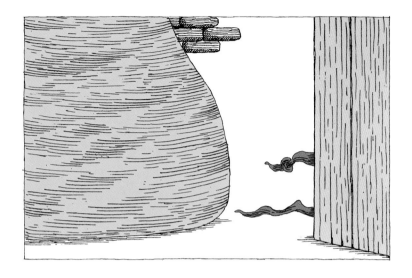

The ugly little man did as directed. When a
distant rooster greeted the dawn, the room was
full to bursting with spun gold, and Omoline was
alone once more.

"A child," she thought. "I'll never have a child!
The king shall have his gold, and I'll go home to
the mill. What king would want a rough country
girl, with red knuckles and plain manners?" She
further thought: "And if . . . well, it won't happen,
but just if . . . no little leaping, rhyming, misbegotten
creature could take any baby of mine!"

There was now enough gold to last for at least one hundred years. To her astonishment, Leonino made good his promise to Omoline. They were wed in a great ceremony and celebrated all over the kingdom. (The old miller went about boasting of how he'd arranged his daughter's marriage.) King and queen ruled side by side, just and wise by day, tender and laughing by night.

A summer passed, and a winter; and in the
spring Queen Omoline brought forth a beautiful
daughter. They named her Arthurina, for the
king's father.

She had nearly put from her mind the creature
who had saved her life and, in a way, made her
queen; but in an obscure corner of her memory
she was always a little afraid. So when, one
dark November afternoon, she heard a familiar
rasping voice, she almost dropped her baby,
with whom she had been playing an interesting
finger-wiggling game.

"Well met, Your Highness! Did you miss me?"
The little man was hanging one-handed from a
bell-pull; as Omoline turned, startled,
he twirled softly to the
nursery floor.

"O what a pretty, pretty baby!" He smirked up at
Arthurina in her lacy linen swaddle. "Fat one, isn't
it?—you do recall our bargain, of course."

Something about the little man—his offhand
confidence, or the icy light in his strange black
eyes—frightened Omoline very badly. "Well—well,
but—" There was a shiver in her voice. "I, I'm
afraid that circumstances have changed." The
little man's toothy smile became something that
was not a smile. "I, I, *you can't have my baby.*"

"A bargain is a bargain. Or are you a liar like
your old father?"

"No, I, but you can't—"

"You promised that baby to me. It's mine. Hand
it over."

"Take my queenly jewels! Take my crown of sapphires! Take *me*, but spare my blameless baby girl!"

This made the little man stop and think. He pulled his long, pale nose and squinted.

"I'm owed a baby, but I love a wager. So here's one: Tell me my name. Tell it right and I'll trouble you no more. Tell it wrong, and I take the baby and yourself as well—they always want help in the kitchen, Down Below."

His eyes were bright and black as jet, his smile a wolf's. "You may try to name me tomorrow night, and the next night, and the night after that—try all the names you can think of. But if you don't guess my name on the third night, you must

Say farewell to your
    throne and your love,
And your merry green
    country here above."

And he sidled out the door.

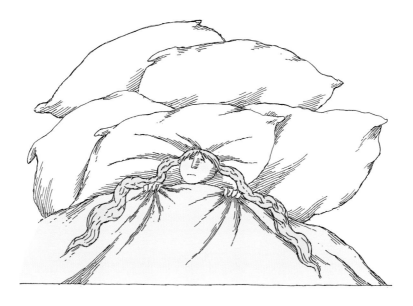

Leaving Arthurina in the care of two large, fierce nurses, the queen went to bed. She tossed and turned and worried. In the morning she called for her courier, a fellow named Zebra.

"I need names," she said, "and quickly. Lope about the south country, Zebra, and learn people's names. Write them down. Bring me a list before sundown." Zebra nodded and loped away.

Pale and quaking, list in hand,
Queen Omoline found the
little man that evening in
her chambers. "Cheerio,
Miss Millwheel," said the
disrespectful gnome.
"Name me, can you?"

Omoline began with the kingdom's
most common names. "Are you
Armsby, Barmsby, Collop,
Drago, Egismund, or
Feeney?" The little man
shook his head, smug.
"Galloon, Hortipher,
Inglenook, Jeeps, Kidneigh,
Lupinaster?" No.

"Mangle, Noodlington,
Octumber, Pettiflap,
Quackus, Roygedowdy,
Sporkazola?" The little man
examined his fingernails,
enjoying himself very much.

"Turlock, Uvula,
Venividivici, Wobshire,
Xtine, Yipple, Zut?"
No, no, no, no, no, no, no.

The queen went on
grimly, and the little man
went on saying no; and
at length the night-bell
rang midnight, and he
was gone.

Another sleepless night followed, and at daybreak Omoline called her courier again. "This time, you must lope and listen in the north country," she instructed him. He returned that evening, footsore, with a new list of names.

Queen Omoline sent the weary Zebra right out
again: "Take a crew, and canvass in the east
and the west. Lope the deep woods and the high
mountains." Later, she carried the new list to her
chambers without a bite of supper—who could
eat?—or a word to her poor puzzled king.

The little man was seated carelessly in the most comfortable chair. Omoline resumed: "Agarunt, Bloykes, Calfspittle?" The little man made a show of being bored. "Deemster, Eekopoulos, Footling, Grossmaple . . ."

The little man found some crumbs in the carpet and ate them.

The evening wore on.
"Wheepsney, Xorsting,
Yordleham, Zoopalon . . ."
No, no, no, no.

The little man laughed
in her face.

"See you tomorrow
night!"—and he
vanished.

Despair in her heart, the queen was staring hopelessly into her looking-glass the next morning when word came that Zebra had returned. "So soon!" she thought, and went down to question him.

"My men are still out gathering names, Majesty," he said. "But I witnessed something very strange in the small hours, something that may interest you; but I don't know whether it's a name or not. Certainly not a name I've ever heard be—" Omoline was generally gracious, but now she interrupted her runner impatiently. "Zebra! Hush up and tell me!"

"I was high in the mountains and deep in the woods—not many people there, but they have strange names. And so I saw a light, and thought I might warm my—"

"To the point, Zebra!"

"So I saw a little fire. And what do I see next but a little man, leaping and capering and dancing around it. And this little man is singing as well, and I can't say as I liked that song—"

"*Zebra!*"

"What he was singing, Queen, was:

'Away down a hole, away Down Below,
Never sorrow over milk that's spilt! Spin
Around, go to ground, take a baby,
    leave a crown,
Just a job o' work to Rumpelstiltskin!'"

Omoline was much cheered to hear Zebra's
report. She left him to doctor his blisters and ran
with a light step to the nursery, where she and
Arthurina had a comfortable time
playing together.

And later she sat in her chambers, watching
the long November twilight deepen into black.
She heard a bump and quickly lit a candle or
two; the little man emerged confidently from
a shadowy corner and took a seat, eager to
conclude the game.

But Omoline felt confident, too. She rattled off
a few dozen new names—Houndsbreadth,
Chumbake, Misgruntle, etc.—from Zebra's list as
the little man smiled and smiled. Then, smiling
herself, she asked innocently, "Do you like your
chair? They call the upholstery *rumpled storkskin*."
A troubled crease appeared
on the little man's brow.
"It's awfully rich
for a *humble
bumpkin* like me."
He cleared his
throat. "No opinion?
Well, I only meant to tell
you to be careful—I think
I lost my *purple stickpin* in that chair."

The little man opened his mouth, then shut it
again, looking foolish. "But let me return to my
guessing," said the queen. "Could your name
be Crumble Skunkstink?" The little man's eyes
slid left and right and left. "Is it ... Trample
Stackscone?" The little man began to writhe
and to tug at his fingers. "Wimple Pluckstring?
Spangle Pigstain? Is it Simple Rumpsplint?" The
little man looked as if he would very much
prefer to be somewhere else.

"Could it be RUMPELSTILTSKIN?"

The little man made a noise like a cat symphony, like a hurricane in a jug, like a thousand large men all sneezing at once. He shot out of his easy chair and threw himself, purple-faced, about the room. Coming to rest at last, he glared terribly at Omoline.

"I will not have this!" he shrieked; and he stamped his right foot, and his left; but when he brought his right foot down once more, the stone floor gave way. The little man's foot disappeared into a jagged, smoke-ringed hole. In an instant, something beyond or beneath the hole seemed to suck him down, still shrieking.

And when King Leonino, surprised by the noise
as he brought little Arthurina for a good-night
kiss from her mama, stuck his head around
the door, he found his queen, alone, looking at a
small hole in the floor. The hole became smaller
as he watched, astonished; then, with a last puff
of oily black smoke, it closed altogether.

And he never did find out what had been going
on in Omoline's chambers: She put him off with
a smile and a kiss, and he quickly forgot all
about it.

And all this happened long ago, but no one has
ever seen that little man since.

Other Edward Gorey books published by Pomegranate:

The Awdrey-Gore Legacy

The Black Doll: A Silent Screenplay by Edward Gorey

The Blue Aspic

Category

The Dong with a Luminous Nose,
   text by Edward Lear

The Eclectic Abecedarium

Edward Gorey: The New Poster Book

Elegant Enigmas: The Art of Edward Gorey,
   by Karen Wilkin

Elephant House: or, the Home of Edward Gorey,
   by Kevin McDermott

The Gilded Bat

The Hapless Child

The Jumblies,
   text by Edward Lear

The Remembered Visit

The Sopping Thursday
The Twelve Terrors of Christmas,
    text by John Updike
The Utter Zoo
The Wuggly Ump

and don't miss:

The Fantod Pack
Edward Gorey's Dracula: A Toy Theatre
The Wuggly Ump and Other Delights Coloring Book